Julia A. J. Foote

A Brand Plucked from the Fire

Julia A. J. Foote

A Brand Plucked from the Fire

ISBN/EAN: 9783743394582

Manufactured in Europe, USA, Canada, Australia, Japa

Cover: Foto ©Raphael Reischuk / pixelio.de

Manufactured and distributed by brebook publishing software
(www.brebook.com)

Julia A. J. Foote

A Brand Plucked from the Fire

PREFACE.

I HAVE written this little book after many prayers to ascertain the will of God—having long had an impression to do it. I have a consciousness of obedience to the will of my dear Lord and Master.

My object has been to testify more extensively to the sufficiency of the blood of Jesus Christ to save from all sin. Many have not the means of purchasing large and expensive works on this important Bible theme.

Those who are fully in the truth cannot possess a prejudiced or sectarian spirit. As they hold fellowship with Christ, they cannot reject those whom he has received, nor receive those whom he rejects, but all are brought nto a blessed harmony with God and each ther.

The Christian who does not believe in salvation from all sin in this life, cannot have a constant, complete peace. The evil of the heart will rise up and give trouble. But let all such remember the words of Paul: "I am crucified with Christ; nevertheless, I live; yet not I, but Christ liveth in me; and the life which I now live in the flesh, I live by faith of the Son of God, who loved me, and gave himself for me." "Ask, and ye shall receive." The blood of Jesus will not only purge your conscience from the guilt of sin, and from dead works, but it will destroy the very root of sin that is in the heart, by faith, so that you may serve the living God in the beauty of holiness.

My earnest desire is that many—especially of my own race—may be led to believe and enter into rest; "For we which have believed do enter into rest"—sweet soul rest.

INTRODUCTION.

The author of this sketch is well known in many parts of Ohio, and in other days was known in several States, as an Evangelist. The purity of her life and the success of her labors are acknowledged. After severe mental and spiritual conflicts, she obeyed God, in public labor for his cause, and still continues in this, although, with many, she is thereby guilty of three great crimes.

1. The first is, that of Color. For, though not now the slaves of individual men, our brethren continue to be under the bondage of society. But if there be crime in color, it lies at the door of Him who "hath made of one blood all nations of men for to dwell on all the face of the earth," and who declares himself to be "no respecter of persons." Holiness takes

the prejudice of color out of both the white and the black, and declares that "The [heart's] the standard of the man."

2. In the next place, we see the crime of Womanhood. As though any one, with heart and lips of love, may not speak forth the praises of Him who hath called us out of darkness into light! The "anointing which abideth" unseals all lips, so that in Christ "there is neither male nor female." Praise God forever!

3. In the last place, our sister, as stated, is an Evangelist. We respect the pastoral office highly, for we know the heart of a pastor; but while the regular field-hands are reaping, pray, let Ruth glean, even if "her hap is to light on a part of the field belonging to Boaz."

> "If you cannot, in the harvest,
>   Garner up the richest sheaves,
> Many a grain, both ripe and golden,
>   Will the careless reapers leave;
> Go and glean among the briers,
>   Growing rank against the wall;
> For it may be that their shadow
>   Hides the heaviest wheat of all."

Our dear sister is not a genius. She is simply strong in common sense, and strong in the Lord. Those of us who heard her preach, last year, at Lodi, where she held the almost breathless attention of five thousand people, by the eloquence of the Holy Ghost, know well where is the hiding of her power.

This is a simple narrative of a life of incidents, many of them stirring and strange. We commend it to all; and with it, the soundness of the doctrine and exhortation with which Sister Foote enforces the sublime cause of Holiness.

THOS. K. DOTY.

Christian Harvester Office,
 Cleveland, June, 1879. }

CONTENTS.

8

Plucked from the Fire.

CHAPTER I.

Birth and Parentage.

I was born in 1823, in Schenectady, N. Y.
I was my mother's fourth child. My father
was born free, but was stolen, when a child,
and enslaved. My mother was born a slave,
in the State of New York. She had one very
cruel master and mistress. This man, whom
she was obliged to call master, tied her up and
whipped her because she refused to submit
herself to him, and reported his conduct to
her mistress. After the whipping, he himself
washed her quivering back with strong salt
water. At the expiration of a week she was
sent to change her clothing, which stuck fast
to her back. Her mistress, seeing that she
could not remove it, took hold of the rough
tow-linen under-garment and pulled it off over

her head with a jerk, which took the skin with it, leaving her back all raw and sore.

This cruel master soon sold my mother, and she passed from one person's hands to another's, until she found a comparatively kind master and mistress in Mr. and Mrs. Cheeseman, who kept a public house.

My father endured many hardships in slavery, the worst of which was his constant exposure to all sorts of weather. There being no railroads at that time, all goods and merchandise were moved from place to place with teams, one of which my father drove.

My father bought himself, and then his wife and their first child, at that time an infant. That infant is now a woman, more than seventy years old, and an invalid, dependent upon the bounty of her poor relatives.

I remember hearing my parents tell what first led them to think seriously of their sinful course. One night, as they were on their way home from a dance, they came to a stream of water, which, owing to rain the night previous, had risen and carried away the log crossing. In their endeavor to ford the stream, my mother made a misstep, and came very nearly being drowned, with her babe in her arms. This nearly fatal accident made such

an impression upon their minds that they
said, "We'll go to no more dances;" and they
kept their word. Soon after, they made a
public profession of religion and united with
the M. E. Church. They were not treated as
Christian believers, but as poor lepers. They
were obliged to occupy certain seats in one
corner of the gallery, and dared not come down
to partake of the Holy Communion until the
last white communicant had left the table.

One day my mother and another colored sister waited until all the white people had, as
they thought, been served, when they started
for the communion table. Just as they reached
the lower door, two of the poorer class of white
folks arose to go to the table. At this, a mother
in Israel caught hold of my mother's dress and
said to her, "Don't you know better than to go
to the table when white folks are there?" Ah!
she did know better than to do such a thing
purposely. This was one of the fruits of slavery. Although professing to love the same
God, members of the same church, and expecting to find the same heaven at last, they could
not partake of the Lord's Supper until the
lowest of the whites had been served. Were
they led by the Holy Spirit? Who shall say?
The Spirit of Truth can never be mistaken,
nor can he inspire anything unholy. How

many at the present day profess great spirituality, and even holiness, and yet are deluded by a spirit of error, which leads them to say to the poor and the colored ones among them, "Stand back a little—I am holier than thou."

My parents continued to attend to the ordinances of God as instructed, but knew little of the power of Christ to save; for their spiritual guides were as blind as those they led.

It was the custom, at that time, for all to drink freely of wine, brandy and gin. I can remember when it was customary at funerals, as well as at weddings, to pass around the decanter and glasses, and sometimes it happened that the pall-bearers could scarcely move out with the coffin. When not handed round, one after another would go to the closet and drink as much as they chose of the liquors they were sure to find there. The officiating clergyman would imbibe as freely as any one. My parents kept liquor in the house constantly, and every morning sling was made, and the children were given the bottom of the cup, where the sugar and a little of the liquor was left, on purpose for them. It is no wonder, is it, that every one of my mother's children loved the taste of liquor?

One day, when I was but five years of age, I found the blue chest, where the black bottle was kept, unlocked—an unusual thing. Raising the lid, I took the bottle, put it to my mouth, and drained it to the bottom. Soon after, the rest of the children becoming frightened at my actions, ran and told aunt Giney—an old colored lady living in a part of our house—who sent at once for my mother, who was away working. She came in great haste, and at once pronounced me DRUNK. And so I was—stupidly drunk. They walked with me, and blew tobacco smoke into my face, to bring me to. Sickness almost unto death followed, but my life was spared. I was like a "brand plucked from the burning."

Dear reader, have you innocent children, given you from the hand of God? Children, whose purity rouses all that is holy and good in your nature? Do not, I pray, give to these little ones of God the accursed cup which will send them down to misery and death. Listen to the voice of conscience, the woes of the drunkard, the wailing of poverty-stricken women and children, and touch not the accursed cup. From Sinai come the awful words of Jehovah, "No drunkard shall inherit the kingdom of heaven."

CHAPTER II.

Religious Impressions---Learning the Alphabet.

I DO not remember having any distinct religious impression until I was about eight years old. At this time there was a "big meeting," as it was called, held in the church to which my parents belonged. Two of the ministers called at our house: one had long gray hair and beard, such as I had never seen before. He came to me, placed his hand on my head, and asked me if I prayed. I said, "Yes, sir," but was so frightened that I fell down on my knees before him and began to say the only prayer I knew, "Now I lay me down to sleep." He lifted me up, saying, "You must be a good girl and pray." He prayed for me long and loud. I trembled with fear, and cried as though my heart would break, for I thought he was the Lord, and I must die. After they had gone, my mother talked with me about my soul more than she ever had before, and told me that this preacher

was a good man, but not the Lord; and that,
if I were a good girl, and said my prayers, I
would go to heaven. This gave me great comfort. I stopped crying, but continued to say,
"Now I lay me." A white woman, who came
to our house to sew, taught me the Lord's
prayer. No tongue can tell the joy that filled
my poor heart when I could repeat, "Our
Father, which art in heaven." It has always
seemed to me that I was converted at this
time.

When my father had family worship, which
was every Sunday morning, he used to sing,

> "Lord, in the morning thou shalt hear
> My voice ascending high."

I took great delight in this worship, and
began to have a desire to learn to read the
Bible. There were none of our family able to
read except my father, who had picked up a
little here and there, and who could, by carefully spelling out the words, read a little in
the New Testament, which was a great pleasure to him. My father would very gladly have
educated his children, but there were no
schools where colored children were allowed.
One day, when he was reading, I asked him to
teach me the letters. He replied, "Child, I
hardly know them myself." Nevertheless, he

commenced with "A," and taught me the
alphabet. Imagine, if you can, my childish
glee over this, my first lesson. The children
of the present time, taught at five years of
age, can not realize my joy at being able to
say the entire alphabet when I was nine years
old.

I still continued to repeat the Lord's prayer
and "Now I lay me," &c., but not so often as I
had done months before. Perhaps I had begun
to backslide, for I was but a child, surrounded
by children, and deprived of the proper kind
of teaching. This is my only excuse for not
proving as faithful to God as I should have
done.

Dear children, with enlightened Christian
parents to teach you, how thankful you should
be that "from a child you are able to say that
you have known the Holy Scriptures, which
are able to make you wise unto salvation,
through faith which is in Christ Jesus." I
hope all my young readers will heed the admo-
nition, "Remember now thy Creator in the
days of thy youth," etc. It will save you from
a thousand snares to mind religion young.
God says: "I love those that love me, and
those that seek me early shall find me." Oh!
I am glad that we are never too young to pray,
or too ignorant or too sinful. The younger,

the more welcome. You have nothing to fear, dear children; come right to Jesus.

Why was Adam afraid of the voice of God in the garden? It was not a strange voice; it was a voice he had always loved. Why did he flee away, and hide himself among the trees? It was because he had disobeyed God. Sin makes us afraid of God, who is holy; nothing but sin makes us fear One so good and so kind. It is a sin for children to disobey their parents. The Bible says: "Honor thy father and thy mother." Dear children, honor your parents by loving and obeying them. If Jesus, the Lord of glory, was subject and obedient to his earthly parents, will you not try to follow his example? Lift up your hearts to the dear, loving Jesus, who, when on earth, took little children in his arms, and blessed them. He will help you, if you pray, "Our Father, which art in heaven, thy dear Son, Jesus Christ, my Saviour, did say, 'Suffer little children to come unto me.' I am a little child, and I come to thee. Draw near to me, I pray thee. Hear me, and forgive the many wicked things I have done, and accept my thanks for the many good gifts thou hast given me. Most of all, I thank thee, dear Father, for the gift of thy dear Son, Jesus Christ, who died for me, and for whose sake I pray thee hear my prayer. Amen."

[2]

CHAPTER III.

The Primes---Going to School.

WHEN I was ten years of age I was sent to live in the country with a family by the name of Prime. They had no children, and soon became quite fond of me. I really think Mrs. Prime loved me. She had a brother who was dying with consumption, and she herself was a cripple. For some time after I went there, Mr. John, the brother, was able to walk from his father's house, which was quite near, to ours, and I used to stand, with tears in my eyes, and watch him as he slowly moved across the fields, leaning against the fence to rest himself by the way. I heard them say he could not live much longer, and that worried me dreadfully; and then I used to wonder if he said his prayers. He always treated me kindly, and often stopped to talk with me.

One day, as he started for home, I stepped up to him and said, "Mr. John, do you say your prayers?" and then I began to cry. He looked at me for a moment, then took my hand

in his and said: "Sometimes I pray; do you?"
I answered, " Yes, sir." Then said he, " You
must pray for me"—and turned and left me.
I ran to the barn, fell down on my knees, and
said: "Our Father, who art in heaven, send
that good man to put his hand on Mr. John's
head." I repeated this many times a day as
long as he lived. After his death I heard
them say he died very happy, and had gone to
heaven. Oh, how my little heart leaped for
joy when I heard that Mr. John had gone to
heaven; I was sure the good man had been
there and laid his hand on his head. "Bless
the Lord, O my soul, and all that is within
me praise his holy name," for good men and
good women, who are not afraid to teach dear
children to pray.

The Primes being an old and influential
family, they were able to send me to a country
school, where I was well treated by both teacher
and scholars.

Children were trained very differently in
those days from what they are now. We were
taught to treat those older than ourselves with
great respect. Boys were required to make a
bow, and girls to drop a courtesy, to any person whom they might chance to meet in the
street. Now, many of us dread to meet children almost as much as we do the half-drunken

men coming out of the saloons. Who is to
blame for this? Parents, are you training
your children in the way they should go?
Are you teaching them obedience and respect?
Are you bringing your little ones to Jesus?
Are they found at your side in the house of
God, on Sunday, or are they roving the streets
or fields? Or, what is worse, are they at home
reading books or newspapers that corrupt the
heart, bewilder the mind, and lead down to
the bottomless pit? Father, mother, look on
this picture, and then on the dear children God
has given you to train up for lives of useful-
ness that will fit them for heaven. May the
dear Father reign in and rule over you, is the
prayer of one who desires to meet you all in
heaven.

CHAPTER IV.

My Teacher Hung for Crime.

My great anxiety to read the Testament caused me to learn to spell quite rapidly, and I was just commencing to read when a great calamity came upon us. Our teacher's name was John Van Paten. He was keeping company with a young lady, who repeated to him a remark made by a lady friend of hers, to the effect that John Van Paten was not very smart, and she didn't see why this young lady should wish to marry him. He became very angry, and, armed with a shotgun, proceeded to the lady's house, and shot her dead. She fell, surrounded by her five weeping children. He then started for town, to give himself up to the authorities. On the way he met the woman's husband and told him what he had done. The poor husband found, on reaching home, that John's words were but too true; his wife had died almost instantly.

After the funeral, the bereaved man went to the prison and talked with John and prayed for his conversion until his prayers were answered, and John Van Paten, the murderer, professed faith in Christ.

Finally the day came for the condemned to be publicly hung (they did not plead emotional insanity in those days). Everybody went to the execution, and I with the rest. Such a sight! Never shall I forget the execution of my first school-teacher. On the scaffold he made a speech, which I cannot remember, only that he said he was happy, and ready to die. He sang a hymn, the chorus of which was,

"I am bound for the kingdom ;
Will you go to glory with me?"

clasping his hands, and rejoicing all the while.

The remembrance of this scene left such an impression upon my mind that I could not sleep for many a night. As soon as I fell into a doze, I could see my teacher's head tumbling about the room as fast as it could go; I would waken with a scream, and could not be quieted until some one came and staid with me.

Never since that day have I heard of a person being hung, but a shudder runs through my whole frame, and a trembling seizes me. Oh, what a barbarous thing is the taking of human life, even though it be "a life for a life," as many believe God commands. That was the old dispensation. Jesus said: "A new commandment I give unto you, that ye love one another." Again: "Resist not evil; but whosoever shall smite thee on thy right cheek, turn to him the other also." Living as we do in the Gospel dispensation, may God help us to follow the precepts and example of Him, who, when he was reviled, reviled not again, and in the agony of death prayed: "Father, forgive them, for they know not what they do." Christian men, vote as you pray, that the legalized traffic in ardent spirits may be abolished, and God grant that capital punishment may be banished from our land.

CHAPTER V.

An Undeserved Whipping.

ALL this time the Primes had treated me as though I were their own child. Now my feelings underwent a great change toward them; my dislike for them was greater than my love had been, and this was the reason. One day, Mrs. Prime, having company, sent me to the cellar to bring up some little pound cakes, which she had made a few days previously. There were but two or three left; these I brought to her. She asked me where the rest were. I told her "I didn't know." At this she grew very angry, and said, "I'll make you know, when the company is gone." She, who had always been so kind and motherly, frightened me so by her looks and action that I trembled so violently I could not speak. This was taken as an evidence of my guilt. The dear Lord alone knows how my little heart ached, for I was entirely innocent of the crime laid to my charge. I had no need to steal anything, for I had a plenty of everything there was.

There was a boy working for Mr. Prime that I always thought took the cakes, for I had seen him put his hand into his pocket hastily, and wipe his mouth carefully, if he met any one on his way from the cellar. But what could I do? I could not prove it, and his stout denial was believed as against my unsupported word.

That night I wished over and over again that I could be hung as John Van Paten had been. In the darkness and silence, Satan came to me and told me to go to the barn and hang myself. In the morning I was fully determined to do so. I went to the barn for that purpose, but that boy, whom I disliked very much, was there, and he laughed at me as hard as he could. All at once my weak feelings left me, and I sprang at him in a great rage, such as I had never known before; but he eluded my grasp, and ran away, laughing. Thus was I a second time saved from a dreadful sin.

That day, Mr. and Mrs. Prime, on their return from town, brought a rawhide. This Mrs. Prime applied to my back until she was tired, all the time insisting that I should confess that I took the cakes. This, of course, I could not do. She then put the rawhide up, saying, "I'll use it again to-morrow; I am determined to make you tell the truth."

That afternoon Mrs. Prime went away, leaving me alone in the house. I carried the rawhide out to the wood pile, took the axe, and cut it up into small pieces, which I threw away, determined not to be whipped with that thing again. The next morning I rose very early, before any one else was up in the house, and started for home. It was a long, lonely road, through the woods; every sound frightened me, and made me run for fear some one was after me. When I reached home, I told my mother all that had happened, but she did not say very much about it. In the afternoon Mr. and Mrs. Prime came to the house, and had a long talk with us about the affair. My mother did not believe I had told a falsehood, though she did not say much before me. She told me in after years that she talked very sharply to the Primes when I was not by. They promised not to whip me again, and my mother sent me back with them, very much against my will.

They were as kind to me as ever, after my return, though I did not think so at the time. I was not contented to stay there, and left when I was about twelve years old. The experience of that last year made me quite a hardened sinner. I did not pray very often, and, when I did, something seemed to say to me, "That good man, with the white hair, don't like you any more."

CHAPTER VI.

Varied Experiences—First and Last Dancing.

I HAD grown to be quite a large girl by this time, so that my mother arranged for me to stay at home, do the work, and attend the younger children while she went out to days' work. My older sister went to service, and the entire care of four youngsters devolved upon me—a thing which I did not at all relish.

About this time my parents moved to Albany, where there was an African Methodist Church. My father and mother both joined the church, and went regularly to all the services, taking all the children with them. This was the first time in my life that I was able to understand, with any degree of intelligence,

what religion was. The minister frequently
visited our house, singing, praying, and talking with us all. I was very much wrought
upon by these visits, and began to see such a
beauty in religion that I resolved to serve God
whatever might happen. But this resolution
was soon broken, having been made in my
own strength.

The pomps and vanities of this world began
to engross my attention as they never had
before. I was at just the right age to be led
away by improper acquaintances. I would
gain my mother's consent to visit some of the
girls, and then would go off to a party, and
once went to the theater, the only time I ever
went in my life. My mother found this out,
and punished me so severely that I never had
any desire to go again. Thus I bartered the
things of the kingdom for the fooleries of the
world.

All this time conviction followed me, and
there were times when I felt a faint desire to
serve the Lord; but I had had a taste of the
world, and thought I could not part with its
idle pleasures. The Holy Spirit seemed not
to strive with me; I was apparently left to
take my fill of the world and its pleasures.
Yet I did not entirely forget God. I went to
church, and said my prayers, though not so

often as I had done. I thank my heavenly
Father that he did not quite leave me to my
own self-destruction, but followed me, sometimes embittering my pleasures and thwarting
my schemes of worldly happiness, and most
graciously preserving me from following the
full bent of my inclination.

My parents had at this time a great deal of
trouble with my eldest sister, who would run
away from home and go to dances—a place
forbidden to us all. The first time I ever
attempted to dance was at a quilting, where
the boys came in the evening, and brought
with them an old man to fiddle. I refused
several invitations, fearing my mother might
come or send for me; but, as she did not, I
yielded to the persuasions of the old fiddler,
and went on to the floor with him, to dance.

The last time I made a public effort at
dancing I seemed to feel a heavy hand upon
my arm pulling me from the floor. I was so
frightened that I fell; the people all crowded
around me, asking what was the matter, thinking I was ill. I told them I was not sick, but
that it was wrong for me to dance. Such loud,
mocking laughter as greeted my answer,
methinks is not often heard this side the gates
of torment, and only then when they are
opened to admit a false-hearted professor of

Christianity. They called me a "little Methodist fool," and urged me to try it again. Being shamed into it, I did try it again, but I had taken only a few steps, when I was seized with a smothering sensation, and felt the same heavy grasp upon my arm, and in my ears a voice kept saying, "Repent! repent!" I immediately left the floor and sank into a seat. The company gathered around me, but not with mocking laughter as before; an invisible presence seemed to fill the place. The dance broke up—all leaving very quietly. Thus was I again "plucked as a brand from the burning."

Had I persisted in dancing, I believe God would have smitten me dead on the spot. Dear reader, do you engage in this ensnaring folly of dancing? Reflect a moment; ask yourself, What good is all this dissipation of body and mind? You are ruining your health, squandering your money, and losing all relish for spiritual things. What good does it do you? Does dancing help to make you a . better Christian? Does it brighten your hopes of happiness beyond the grave? The Holy Spirit whispers to your inmost soul, to come out from among the wicked and be separate.

I am often told that the Bible does not condemn dancing—that David danced. Yes, David did dance, but he danced to express his pious joy to the Lord. So Miriam danced, but it was an act of worship, accompanied by a hymn of praise. Herod's daughter, who was a heathen, danced, and her dancing caused the beheading of one of God's servants. Do you find anything in these examples to countenance dancing? No, no; a thousand times, no. Put away your idols, and give God the whole heart.

After the dance to which I have alluded, I spent several days and nights in an agony of prayer, asking God to have mercy on me; but the veil was still upon my heart. Soon after this, there was a large party given, to which our whole family were invited. I did not care to go, but my mother insisted that I should, saying that it would do me good, for I had been moping for several days. So I went to the party. There I laughed and sang, and engaged in all the sports of the evening, and soon my conviction for sin wore away, and foolish amusements took its place.

Mothers, you know not what you do when you urge your daughter to go to parties to make her more cheerful. You may even be causing the eternal destruction of that daughter. God help you, mothers, to do right.

CHAPTER VII.

My Conversion.

I WAS converted when fifteen years old. It was on a Sunday evening at a quarterly meeting. The minister preached from the text: "And they sung as it were a new song before the throne, and before the four beasts and the elders, and no man could learn that song but the hundred and forty and four thousand which were redeemed from the earth." Rev. xiv. 3.

As the minister dwelt with great force and power on the first clause of the text, I beheld my lost condition as I never had done before. Something within me kept saying, "Such a sinner as you are can never sing that new song." No tongue can tell the agony I suffered. I fell to the floor, unconscious, and was carried home. Several remained with me all night, singing and praying. I did not recognize any one, but seemed to be walking in the dark, followed by some one who kept saying, "Such a sinner as you are can never sing that new song." Every converted man and woman

can imagine what my feelings were. I thought
God was driving me on to hell. In great ter-
ror I cried: "Lord, have mercy on me, a poor
sinner!" The voice which had been crying
in my ears ceased at once, and a ray of light
flashed across my eyes, accompanied by a sound
of far distant singing; the light grew brighter
and brighter, and the singing more distinct,
and soon I caught the words: "This is the new
song—redeemed, redeemed!" I at once sprang
from the bed where I had been lying for twenty
hours, without meat or drink, and commenced
singing: "Redeemed! redeemed! glory! glory!"
Such joy and peace as filled my heart, when I
felt that I was redeemed and could sing the
new song. Thus was I wonderfully saved from
eternal burning.

I hastened to take down the Bible, that I
might read of the new song, and the first words
that caught my eye were: "But now, thus saith
the Lord that created thee, O Jacob, and he
that formed thee, O Israel, fear not, for I have
redeemed thee; I have called thee by thy
name; thou art mine. When thou passest
through the waters, I will be with thee, and
through the rivers they shall not overflow
thee; when thou walkest through the fire,
thou shalt not be burned, neither shall the
flame kindle upon thee." Isaiah xliii. 1, 2.

[3]

My soul cried, "Glory! glory!" and I was
filled with rapture too deep for words. Was I
not indeed a brand plucked from the burning?
I went from house to house, telling my young
friends what a dear Saviour I had found, and
that he had taught me the new song. Oh!
how memory goes back to those childish days
of innocence and joy.

Some of my friends laughed at me, and said:
"We have seen you serious before, but it didn't
last long." I said: "Yes, I have been serious
before, but I could never sing the new song
until now."

One week from the time of my conversion,
Satan tempted me dreadfully, telling me I was
deceived; people didn't get religion in that
way, but went to the altar, and were prayed
for by the minister. This seemed so very
reasonable that I began to doubt if I had
religion. But, in the first hour of this doubting, God sent our minister in to talk with me.
I told him how I was feeling, and that I feared
I was not converted. He replied: "My child,
it is not the altar nor the minister that saves
souls, but faith in the Lord Jesus Christ, who
died for all men." Taking down the Bible, he
read: "By grace are ye saved, through faith,
and that not of yourselves; it is the gift of
God." He asked me then if I believed my

sins had all been forgiven, and that the
Saviour loved me.   I replied that I believed it
with all my heart.   No tongue can express the
joy that came to me at that moment.   There
is great peace in believing. Glory to the
Lamb!

———————•———————

CHAPTER VIII.

A Desire for Knowledge—Inward Foes.

I STUDIED the Bible at every spare moment,
that I might be able to read it with a better
understanding.   I used to read at night by
the light of the dying fire, after the rest of the
family had gone to bed.   One night I dropped
the tongs, which made such a noise that my
mother came to see what was the matter.
When she found that I had been in the habit
of reading at night, she was very much displeased, and took the Bible away from me, and
would not allow me to have it at such times
any more.

Soon after this, my minister made me a
present of a new Bible and Testament.   Had
he given me a thousand dollars, I should not

have cared for it as I did for this Bible. I
cherished it tenderly, but did not read in it at
night, for I dared not disobey my mother.

I now felt the need of an education more
than ever. I was a poor reader and a poor
writer; but the dear Holy Spirit helped me by
quickening my mental faculties. O Lord, I
will praise thee, for great is thy goodness! Oh,
that everything that hath a being would praise
the Lord! From this time, Satan never had
power to make me doubt my conversion. Bless
God! I knew in whom I believed.

For six months I had uninterrupted peace
and joy in Jesus, my love. At the end of that
time an accident befell me, which aroused a
spirit within me such as I had not known that
I possessed. One day, as I was sitting at work,
my younger brother, who was playing with
the other small children, accidentally hit me
in the eye, causing the most intense suffering.
The eye was so impaired that I lost the sight
of it. I was very angry; and soon pride, impa-
tience, and other signs of carnality, gave me a
great deal of trouble. Satan said: "There!
you see you never were converted." But he
could not make me believe that, though I did
not know the cause of these repinings within.

I went to God with my troubles, and felt
relieved for a while; but they returned again

and again. Again I went to the Lord, earnestly striving to find what was the matter. I knew what was right, and tried to do right, but when I would do good, evil was present with me. Like Gad, I was weak and feeble, having neither might, wisdom nor ability to overcome my enemies or maintain my ground without many a foil. Yet, never being entirely defeated, disabled or vanquished, I would gather fresh courage, and renew the fight. Oh, that I had then had some one to lead me into the light of full salvation!

But instead of getting light, my preacher, class-leader, and parents, told me that all Christians had these inward troubles to contend with, and were never free from them until death; that this was my work here, and I must keep fighting and that, when I died, God would give me a bright crown. What delusion! However, I believed my minister was too good and too wise not to know what was right; so I kept on struggling and fighting with this inbeing monster, hoping all the time I should soon die and be at rest—never for a moment supposing I could be cleansed from all sin, and live.

I had heard of the doctrine of Holiness, but in such a way as to give me no light, nor to beget a power in me to strive after the experience. How frivolous and fruitless is that preaching which describes the mere history of the work and has not the power of the Holy Ghost. My observation has shown me that there are many, ah! too many shepherds now, who live under the dreadful woe pronounced by the Lord upon the shepherds of Israel (Ezekiel xxxiv.).

CHAPTER IX.

Various Hopes Blasted.

THE more my besetting sin troubled me, the more anxious I became for an education. I believed that, if I were educated, God could make me understand what I needed; for, in spite of what others said, it would come to me, now and then, that I needed something more than what I had, but what that something was I could not tell.

About this time Mrs. Phileos and Miss Crandall met with great indignity from a pro-slavery mob in Canterbury, Conn., because they dared to teach colored children to read. If they went out to walk, they were followed by a rabble of men and boys, who hooted at them, and threw rotten eggs and other missiles at them, endangering their lives and frightening them terribly.

One scholar, with whom I was acquainted, was so frightened that she went into spasms, which resulted in a derangement from which she never recovered. We were a despised and oppressed people; we had no refuge but God. He heard our cries, saw our tears, and wonderfully delivered us.

Bless the Lord that he is "a man of war!" "I am that I am" is his name. Mr. and Mrs. Phileos and their daughter opened a school in Albany for colored children of both sexes. This was joyful news to me. I had saved a little money from my earnings, and my father promised to help me; so I started with hopes, expecting in a short time to be able to understand the Bible, and read and write well. Again was I doomed to disappointment: for some inexplicable reason, the family left the place in a few weeks after beginning the school. My poor heart sank within me. I could scarcely speak for constant weeping. That was my last schooling. Being quite a young woman, I was obliged to work, and study the Bible as best I could. The dear Holy Spirit helped me wonderfully to understand the precious Word.

Through temptation I was brought into
great distress of mind; the enemy of souls
thrust sore at me; but I was saved from fall-
ing into his snares—saved in the hour of trial
from my impetuous spirit, by the angel of the
Lord standing in the gap, staying me in my
course.

"Oh, bless the name of Jesus! he maketh the rebel a
priest and king;
He hath bought me and taught me the new song to sing."

I continued to live in an up-and-down way
for more than a year, when there came to our
church an old man and his wife, who, when
speaking in meeting, told of the trouble they
once had had in trying to overcome their temper, subdue their pride, etc. But they took all
to Jesus, believing his blood could wash them
clean and sanctify them wholly to himself;
and, oh! the peace, the sweet peace, they had
enjoyed ever since. Their words thrilled me
through and through.

I at once understood what I needed. Though
I had read in my Bible many things they told
me, I had never understood what I read. I
needed a Philip to teach me.

I told my parents, my minister, and my
leader that I wanted to be sanctified. They
told me sanctification was for the aged and
persons about to die, and not for one like me.

All they said did me no good. I had wandered
in the wilderness a long time, and now that I
could see a ray of the light for which I had so
long sought, I could not rest day nor night
until I was free.

I wanted to go and visit these old people
who had been sanctified, but my mother said:
"No, you can't go; you are half crazy now, and
these people don't know what they are talking
about." To have my mother refuse my request
so peremptorily made me very sorrowful for
many days. Darkness came upon me, and my
distress was greater than before, for, instead of
following the true light, I was turned away
from it.

CHAPTER X.

Disobedience, but Happy Results.

FINALLY, I did something I never had done before : I deliberately disobeyed my mother. I visited these old saints, weeping as though my heart would break. When I grew calm, I told them all my troubles, and asked them what I must do to get rid of them. They told me that sanctification was for the young believer, as well as the old. These words were a portion in due season. After talking a long time, and they had prayed with me, I returned home, though not yet satisfied.

I remained in this condition more than a week, going many times to my secret place of prayer, which was behind the chimney in the garret of our house. None but those who have passed up this way know how wretched every moment of my life was. I thought I must die. But truly, God does make his little ones ministering angels—sending them forth on missions of love and mercy. So he sent that dear old mother in Israel to me one fine morning in May. At the sight of her my heart seemed to

melt within me, so unexpected, and yet so
much desired was her visit. Oh, bless the
Lord for sanctified men and women!

There was no one at home except the
younger children, so our coming together was
uninterrupted. She read and explained many
passages of Scripture to me, such as, John
xvii; 1 Thess. iv. 3; v. 23; 1 Cor. vi. 9–12;
Heb. ii. 11; and many others—carefully mark-
ing them in my Bible. All this had been as a
sealed book to me until now. Glory to Jesus!
the seals were broken and light began to shine
upon the blessed Word of God as I had never
seen it before.

The second day after that pilgrim's visit,
while waiting on the Lord, my large desire
was granted, through faith in my precious
Saviour. The glory of God seemed almost to
prostrate me to the floor. There was, indeed,
a weight of glory resting upon me. I sang
with all my heart,

> "This is the way I long have sought,
> And mourned because I found it not."

Glory to the Father! glory to the Son! and
glory to the Holy Ghost! who hath plucked
me as a brand from the burning, and sealed
me unto eternal life. I no longer hoped for
glory, but I had the full assurance of it. Praise

the Lord for Paul-like faith! "I am crucified with Christ: nevertheless, I live; yet not I, but Christ liveth in me." This, my constant prayer, was answered, that I might be strengthened with might by his Spirit in the inner man; that being rooted and grounded in love, I might be able to comprehend with all saints what is the length, and breadth, and heighth, and depth, and to know the love of Christ which passeth knowledge, and be filled with all the fullness of God.

I had been afraid to tell my mother I was praying for sanctification, but when the "old man" was cast out of my heart, and perfect love took possession, I lost all fear. I went straight to my mother and told her I was sanctified. She was astonished, and called my father and told him what I had said. He was amazed as well, but said not a word. I at once began to read to them out of my Bible, and to many others, thinking, in my simplicity, that they would believe and receive the same blessing at once. To the glory of God, some did believe and were saved, but many were too wise to be taught by a child—too good to be made better.

From this time, many, who had been my warmest friends, and seemed to think me a Christian, turned against me, saying I did not

know what I was talking about—that there
was no such thing as sanctification and holiness in this life—and that the devil had
deluded me into self-righteousness. Many of
them fought holiness with more zeal and vigor
than they did sin. Amid all this, I had that
sweet peace that passeth all understanding
springing up within my soul like a perennial
fountain—glory to the precious blood of Jesus!

"The King of heaven and earth
Deigns to dwell with mortals here."

CHAPTER XI.

A Religion as Old as the Bible.

THE pastor of our church visited me one day, to talk about my "new religion," as he called it. I took my Bible and read many of my choice passages to him, such as — "Come and hear, all ye that fear God, and I will declare what he hath done for my soul." (Psa. lxvi. 16) "Blessed is he whose transgression is forgiven, whose sin is covered." (Psa. xxxii. 1.) While reading this verse, my whole being was so filled with the glory of God that I exclaimed: "Glory to Jesus! he has freed me from the guilt of sin, and sin hath no longer dominion over me; Christ makes me holy as well as happy."

I also read these words from Ezekiel xxxvi.: "Then will I sprinkle clean water upon you, and ye shall be clean; from all your filthiness and from all your idols will I cleanse you; a new heart also will I give you, and a new spirit will I put within you, and I will take away the stony heart out of your flesh, and I will give you a heart of flesh. And I will put my Spirit within you, and cause you to walk in my statutes, and ye shall keep my judgments, and do them."

I stopped reading, and asked the preacher to explain these last verses to me. He replied: "They are all well enough; but you must remember that you are too young to read and dictate to persons older than yourself, and many in the church are dissatisfied with the way you are talking and acting." As he answered me, the Lord spoke to my heart and glory filled my soul. I said: "My dear minister, I wish they would all go to Jesus, in prayer and faith, and he will teach them as he has taught me." As the minister left me, I involuntarily burst forth into praises:

"My soul is full of glory inspiring my tongue,
  Could I meet with angels I would sing them a song."

Though my gifts were but small, I could not be shaken by what man might think or say.

I continued day by day, month after month, to walk in the light as He is in the light, having fellowship with the Trinity and those aged saints. The blood of Jesus Christ cleansed me from all sin, and enabled me to rejoice in persecution.

Bless the Lord, O my soul, for this wonderful
salvation, that snatched me as a brand from
the burning, even me, a poor, ignorant girl!

And will he not do for all what he did for
me? Yes, yes; God is no respecter of persons.
Jesus' blood will wash away all your sin and
make you whiter than snow.

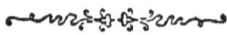

CHAPTER XII.

My Marriage.

Soon after my conversion, a young man,
who had accompanied me to places of amuse-
ment, and for whom I had formed quite an
attachment, professed faith in Christ and
united with the same church to which I
belonged. A few months after, he made me
an offer of marriage. I struggled not a little
to banish the thought from my mind, chiefly
because he was not sanctified. But my feelings were so strongly enlisted that I felt sure
he would some day be my husband. I read to
him and talked to him on the subject of a
cleansed heart. He assented to all my argu-

ments, saying he believed and would seek for it.

The few weeks that he remained with us I labored hard with him for his deliverance, but he left us to go to Boston, Mass. We corresponded regularly, he telling me of his religious enjoyment, but that he did not hear anything about sanctification. Great was my anxiety lest the devil should steal away the good seed out of his heart. The Lord, and he only, knows how many times I besought him to let the clear light of holiness shine into that man's heart. Through all this my mind was stayed upon God; I rested in the will of the Lord.

One night, about a month after his departure, I could not sleep, the tempter being unusually busy with me. Rising, I prostrated myself before the Lord. While thus upon my face, these words of God came to me : "For we have not an high priest which cannot be touched with the feeling of our infirmities; but was in all points tempted like as we are, yet without sin." (Heb. iv. 15.) I at once rose up, thanking God for his precious words : I took my Bible and read them over and over again ; also the eighteenth verse of the second chapter of Hebrews. I was not conscious of having committed sin, and I cried out : "Leave

[4]

me, Satan; I am the Lord's." At that the
tempter left, and I surrendered myself and all
my interests into the hands of God. Glory to
his holy name! "For it pleased the Father
that in him should all fullness dwell," and of
his fullness have I received, and grace for
grace.

> "Praise God from whom all blessings flow,
> Praise him all creatures here below."

The day following this night of temptation
was one of great peace — peace flowing as a
river, even to overflowing its banks, and such
glory of the Lord appeared as to almost deprive
me of bodily powers. I forgot all toil and care.

This was just a year after my heart was
emptied of sin. Through faith I received the
Saviour, and in the same have continued ever
since and proved him able to keep from sin.
Bless God! all my desires are satisfied in him.
He is indeed my reconciled God, the Christ
Jesus whose precious blood is all my righteous-
ness.

> "Nought of good that I have done,
> Nothing but the blood of Jesus."

Glory to the blood that hath bought me!
glory to the blood that hath cleansed me!
glory to the blood that keeps me clean!—me, a
brand plucked from the fire.

George returned in about a year to claim me as his bride. He still gave evidence of being a Christian, but had not been cleansed from the carnal mind. I still continued to pray for his sanctification, and desired that it should take place before our union, but I was so much attached to him that I could not resist his pleadings; so, at the appointed time, we were married, in the church, in the presence of a large number of people, many of whom followed us to my father's house to offer their congratulations.

We staid at home but one day after the ceremony. This day I spent in preparing for our departure and in taking leave of my friends. Tenderly as I loved my parents, much as I loved the church, yet I found myself quite willing to leave them all in the divine appointment.

The day following, accompanied by several friends, we started for Boston, in an old-fashioned stage-coach, there being no railroads at that time. As I rode along I admired the goodness of God, and my heart overflowed with gratitude to him, who had blessed me with power to choose his will and make me able to say with truth, "I gladly forsake all to follow thee."

Once, the thought of leaving my father's

house, to go among strangers, would have been terrible, but now I rejoiced in being so favored as to be called to make this little sacrifice, and evince my love to him who saith : "He that loveth father or mother more than me is not worthy of me."

CHAPTER XIII.

Removal to Boston—The Work of Full Salvation.

ON our arrival in Boston, after a long, wearisome journey, we went at once to the house of Mrs. Burrows, where my husband had made arrangements for me to board while he was away at work during the week. He worked in Chelsea, and could not come to look after my welfare but once a week. The boarders in this house were mostly gentlemen, nearly all of whom were out of Christ. Mrs. Burrows was a church-member, but knew nothing of the full joys of salvation.

I went to church the first Sabbath I was there, remained at class-meeting, gave my letter of membership to the minister, and was received into the church. In giving my first testimony, I told of my thorough and happy conversion, and of my sanctification as a second, distinct work of the Holy Ghost.

After class-meeting, a good many came to me, asking questions about sanctification; others stood off in groups, talking, while a few followed me to my boarding-house. They all seemed very much excited over what I had told them. I began to see that it was not the voice of man that had bidden me go out from the land of my nativity and from my kindred, but the voice of my dear Lord. I was completely prepared for all that followed, knowing that "All things work together for good to them that love God." Change of people, places and circumstances, weighed nothing with me, for I had a safe abiding place with my Father. Some people had been to me in such an unchristianlike spirit that I had spoken to and about them in rather an incautious manner. I now more and more saw the great need of ordering all my words as in the immediate presence of God, that I might be able to maintain that purity of lips and life which the Gospel required. God is holy, and if I would enjoy constant communion with him I must guard every avenue of my soul, and watch

every thought of my heart and word of my
tongue, that I may be blameless before him in
love. The Lord help me evermore to be upon
my guard, and having done all, to stand.
Amen and amen.

In a few months my husband rented a house
just across the road from my boarding-house,
and I went to housekeeping. "Mam" Riley,
a most excellent Christian, became as a mother
to me in this strange land, far from my own
dear mother. Bless the Lord! He supplied
all my needs. "Mam" Riley had two grown
daughters, one about my own age, married,
who had two children. They were dear Christian women, and like sisters to me. The
mother thought she once enjoyed the blessing
of heart purity, but the girls had not heard of
such a thing as being sanctified and permitted
to live. The elder girl, who was a consump-
tive and in delicate health, soon became deeply
interested in the subject. She began to hun-
ger and thirst after righteousness, and did not
rest until she was washed and made clean in
the blood of Jesus. Her clear, definite testimony had a great effect upon the church, as
her family was one of the first in point of
wealth and standing in the community.

God wonderfully honored the faith of this
young saint in her ceaseless labor for others.

We attended meetings and visited from house to house, together, almost constantly, when she was able to go out. Glory to God! the church became much aroused; some plunged into the ocean of perfect love, and came forth testifying to the power of the blood. Others disbelieved and ridiculed this "foolish doctrine," as they called it, saying it was just as impossible to live without committing sin as it was to live without eating, and brought disjointed passages of Scripture to bear them out.

CHAPTER XIV.

Early Fruit Gathered Home.

AFTER I went to Boston I was much drawn out in prayer for the sanctification of believers. Notwithstanding the enemy labored by various means to hinder the work of grace, yet the Lord wrought a wonderful change in many.

The mother of my friend received a fresh baptism, and came back into the light, praising the Lord. That the Holy Spirit might keep my dear "Mam" Riley pure until death, was my prayer.

· The health of my dear friend, Mrs. Simpson, began rapidly to fail. One morning, in reply to my question as to her health, she said: "Dear sister, I have been in great pain through the night, but you know Jesus said, 'I will never leave thee nor forsake thee.' Praise God, who has been with me in great mercy through the darkness of the night." I remained with her the following night, and such calmness, patience and resignation through suffering, I never had witnessed. Toward morning she was more easy, and asked for her husband.

When he came, she embraced him, repeated passages of Scripture to him, and exhorted him, as she had many times before, to receive God in all his fullness.

There, in that death-chamber, in the stillness of night, we prayed for that pious and exemplary man, that he might present his body a living sacrifice. He was deeply moved upon by the Holy Spirit, so that he cried aloud for deliverance; but almost on the instant began to doubt, and left the room. His wife requested me to read and talk to her about Jesus, which I did, and she was filled with heavenly joy and shouted aloud: "Oh, the blood, the precious blood of Jesus cleanses me now!"

Her mother, who was sleeping in an adjoining room, was awakened by the noise and came in, saying, as she did so: "This room is filled with the glory of God. Hallelujah! Amen."

As the morning dawned, Mrs. Simpson sank into a quiet slumber, which lasted several hours. She awoke singing:

"How happy are they who their Saviour obey,
And have laid up their treasure above."

She was comparatively free from pain for several days, though very weak. She talked to all who came to see her of salvation free and full. Her last morning on earth came. She was peaceful and serene, with a heavenly smile upon her countenance. She asked me to pray, which I did with streaming eyes and quivering voice. She then asked us to sing the hymn,

"Oh, for a thousand tongues to sing
My great Redeemer's praise."

She sang with us in a much stronger voice than she had used for many days. As we sang the last verse, she raised herself up in bed, clapped her hands and cried: "He sets the prisoner free! Glory! glory! I am free! They have come for me!" She pointed toward the east. Her mother asked her who had come.

She said: "Don't you see the chariot and horses? Glory! glory to the blood!"

She dropped back upon her pillow, and was gone. She had stepped aboard the chariot, which we could not see, but we felt the fire.

While many in the room were weeping, her mother shed not a tear, but shouted, "Glory to God!" Then, with her own hands, she assisted in arranging and preparing the remains for burial. Thus did another sanctified saint enter into eternal life. Though her period of sanctification was short, it was full of precious fruit.

CHAPTER XV.

New and Unpleasant Revelations.

My husband had always treated the subject
of heart purity with favor, but now he began
to speak against it. He said I was getting
more crazy every day, and getting others in
the same way, and that if I did not stop he
would send me back home or to the crazy-
house. I questioned him closely respecting
the state of his mind, feeling that he had been
prejudiced. I did not attempt to contend with
him on the danger and fallacy of his notions,
but simply asked what his state of grace was,
if God should require his soul of him then.
He gave me no answer until I insisted upon
one. Then he said: "Julia, I don't think I
can ever believe myself as holy as you think
you are."

I then urged him to believe in Christ's holiness, if he had no faith in the power of the
blood of Christ to cleanse from all sin. He

that hath this hope purifies himself as God is
pure. We knelt in prayer together, my husband leading, and he seemed much affected
while praying. To me it was a precious season, though there was an indescribable something between us—something dark and high.
As I looked at it, these words of the poet came
to me:

"God moves in a mysterious way,
His wonders to perform."

From that time I never beheld my husband's face clear and distinct, as before, the
dark shadow being ever present. This caused
me not a little anxiety and many prayers.
Soon after, he accepted an offer to go to sea for
six months, leaving me to draw half of his
wages. To this arrangement I reluctantly
consented, fully realizing how lonely I should
be among strangers. Had it not been for dear
"Mam" Riley, I could hardly have endured it.
Her precept and example taught me to lean
more heavily on Christ for support. God gave
me these precious words: "Be careful for nothing, but in everything, by prayer and supplication, with thanksgiving, let your requests be
made known unto God." Truly, God is the
great Arbiter of all events, and "because he
lives, I shall live also."

The day my husband went on ship-board was one of close trial and great inward temptation. It was difficult for me to mark the exact line between disapprobation and Christian forbearance and patient love. How I longed for wisdom to meet everything in a spirit of meekness and fear, that I might not be surprised into evil or hindered from improving all things to the glory of God.

While under this apparent cloud, I took the Bible to my closet, asking Divine aid. As I opened the book, my eyes fell on these words: "For thy Maker is thine husband." I then read the fifty-fourth chapter of Isaiah over and over again. It seemed to me that I had never seen it before. I went forth glorifying God.

CHAPTER XVI.

A Long-Lost Brother Found.

HAVING no children, I had a good deal of leisure after my husband's departure, so I visited many of the poor and forsaken ones, reading and talking to them of Jesus, the Saviour. One day I was directed by the Spirit to visit the Marine Hospital. In passing through one of the wards I heard myself called by my maiden name. Going to the cot from whence the voice came, I beheld what seemed to me a human skeleton. As I looked I began to see our family likeness, and recognized my eldest brother, who left home many years before, when I was quite young. Not hearing from him, we had mourned him as dead. With a feeble voice, he told me of his roving and seafaring life; "and now, sister," he said, "I am dying."

I asked him if he was willing to die—if he was ready to stand before God. "No, oh, no!" he said. I entreated him to pray. He shook his head, saying, "I can't pray; my heart is too hard, and my mind dark and bewildered," and then cried out, in the agony of his soul, "Oh, that dreadful, burning hell! how can I escape it?"

I urged him to pray, and to believe that Jesus died for all. I prayed for him, and staid with him as much as possible. One morning, when I went to see him, I was shown his lifeless remains in the dead-house. This was, indeed, a solemn time for me.

I had very little hope in my brother's death. But there is an High Priest who ever liveth to make intercession for all, and I trust that he prevailed. The Lord is the Judge of all the earth, and all souls are in his hands, and he will in no wise clear the guilty, though merciful and wise. Willful unbelief is a crying sin, and will not be passed by without punishment. God judges righteously, and is the avenger of all sin. Justice is meted out to all, either here or in eternity. Praise the Lord! My whole soul joins in saying, Praise the Lord!

God, in great mercy, returned my husband to me in safety, for which I bowed in great thankfulness. George told me that the ship was a poor place to serve the Lord, and that the most he heard was oaths. He said that sometimes he would slip away and pray, and that, upon one occasion, the captain came upon him unawares, and called him "a fool," and told him to get up and go to work. Notwithstanding all this, my husband shipped for a second voyage. Praise the Lord! he saved me from a painful feeling at parting. With joy could I say, "Thou everywhere-present God! thy will be done."

During the year I had been from home, letters from my parents and friends had come to me quite often, filling me with gladness and thanksgiving for the many blessings and cheering words they contained. But now a letter came bringing the intelligence that my family were about to move to Silver Lake, which was much farther from me. I tremblingly went to my heavenly Father, who gave me grace and strength at once.

CHAPTER XVII.

My Call to Preach the Gospel.

FOR months I had been moved upon to exhort and pray with the people, in my visits from house to house; and in meetings my whole soul seemed drawn out for the salvation of souls. The love of Christ in me was not limited. Some of my mistaken friends said I was too forward, but a desire to work for the Master, and to promote the glory of his kingdom in the salvation of souls, was food to my poor soul.

When called of God, on a particular occasion, to a definite work, I said, "No, Lord, not me." Day by day I was more impressed that God would have me work in his vineyard. I thought it could not be that I was called to preach—I, so weak and ignorant. Still, I knew all things were possible with God, even to confounding the wise by the foolish things of this earth. Yet in me there was a shrinking.

[5]

I took all my doubts and fears to the Lord in prayer, when, what seemed to be an angel, made his appearance. In his hand was a scroll, on which were these words: "Thee have I chosen to preach my Gospel without delay." The moment my eyes saw it, it appeared to be printed on my heart. The angel was gone in an instant, and I, in agony, cried out, "Lord, I cannot do it!" It was eleven o'clock in the morning, yet everything grew dark as night. The darkness was so great that I feared to stir.

At last "Mam" Riley entered. As she did so, the room grew lighter, and I arose from my knees. My heart was so heavy I scarce could speak. Dear "Mam" Riley saw my distress, and soon left me.

From that day my appetite failed me and sleep fled from my eyes. I seemed as one tormented. I prayed, but felt no better. I belonged to a band of sisters whom I loved dearly, and to them I partially opened my mind. One of them seemed to understand my case at once, and advised me to do as God had bid me, or I would never be happy here or hereafter. But it seemed too hard—I could not give up and obey.

One night, as I lay weeping and beseeching the dear Lord to remove this burden from me, there appeared the same angel that came to me before, and on his breast were these words: "You are lost unless you obey God's righteous commands." I saw the writing, and that was enough. I covered my head and awoke my husband, who had returned a few days before. He asked me why I trembled so, but I had not power to answer him. I remained in that condition until morning, when I tried to arise and go about my usual duties, but was too ill. Then my husband called a physician, who prescribed medicine, but it did me no good.

I had always been opposed to the preaching of women, and had spoken against it, though, I acknowledge, without foundation. This rose before me like a mountain, and when I thought of the difficulties they had to encounter, both from professors and non-professors, I shrank back and cried, "Lord, I cannot go!"

The trouble my heavenly Father has had to keep me out of the fire that is never quenched, he alone knoweth. My husband and friends said I would die or go crazy if something favorable did not take place soon. I expected to die and be lost, knowing I had been enlightened and had tasted the heavenly gift. I read again and again the sixth chapter of Hebrews.

CHAPTER XVIII.

Heavenly Visitations Again.

NEARLY two months from the time I first saw the angel, I said that I would do anything or go anywhere for God, if it were made plain to me. He took me at my word, and sent the angel again with this message: "You have I chosen to go in my name and warn the people of their sins." I bowed my head and said, "I will go, Lord."

That moment I felt a joy and peace I had not known for months. But strange as it may appear, it is not the less true, that, ere one hour had passed, I began to reason thus:"I am elected to preach the Gospel without the requisite qualifications, and, besides, my parents and friends will forsake me and turn against me; and I regret that I made a promise." At that instant all the joy and peace I had felt left me, and I thought I was standing on the brink of hell, and heard the devil say: "Let her go! let her go! I will catch her." Reader,

can you imagine how I felt? If you were ever
snatched from the mouth of hell, you can, in
part, realize my feelings.

I continued in this state for some time,
when, on a Sabbath evening—ah! that memo-
rable Sabbath evening—while engaged in fer-
vent prayer, the same supernatural presence
came to me once more and took me by the
hand. At that moment I became lost to
everything of this world. The angel led me
to a place where there was a large tree, the
branches of which seemed to extend either
way beyond sight. Beneath it sat, as I thought,
God the Father, the Son, and the Holy Spirit,
besides many others, whom I thought were
angels. I was led before them : they looked
me over from head to foot, but said nothing.
Finally, the Father said to me : "Before these
people make your choice, whether you will
obey me or go from this place to eternal misery
and pain." I answered not a word. He then
took me by the hand to lead me, as I thought,
to hell, when I cried out, "I will obey thee,
Lord!" He then pointed my hand in different directions, and asked if I would go there.
I replied, "Yes, Lord." He then led me, all
the others following, till we came to a place
where there was a great quantity of water,
which looked like silver, where we made a

halt. My hand was given to Christ, who led me into the water and stripped me of my clothing, which at once vanished from sight. Christ then appeared to wash me, the water feeling quite warm.

During this operation, all the others stood on the bank, looking on in profound silence. When the washing was ended, the sweetest music I had ever heard greeted my ears. We walked to the shore, where an angel stood with a clean, white robe, which the Father at once put on me. In an instant I appeared to be changed into an angel. The whole company looked at me with delight, and began to make a noise which I called shouting. We all marched back with music. When we reached the tree to which the angel first led me, it hung full of fruit, which I had not seen before. The Holy Ghost plucked some and gave me, and the rest helped themselves. We sat down and ate of the fruit, which had a taste like nothing I had ever tasted before. When we had finished, we all arose and gave another shout. Then God the Father said to me: "You are now prepared, and must go where I have commanded you." I replied, "If I go, they will not believe me." Christ then appeared to write something with a golden pen and golden ink, upon golden paper. Then he rolled it up, and said to me : "Put this in .your bosom, and, wherever you go, show it, and they will know that I have sent you to proclaim salvation to all." He then put it into my bosom, and they all went with me to a bright, shining gate, singing and shouting. Here they embraced me, and I found myself once more on earth.

When I came to myself, I found that several friends had been with me all night, and my husband had called a physician, but he had not been able to do anything for me. He ordered those around me to keep very quiet, or to go home. He returned in the morning, when I told him, in part, my story. He seemed amazed, but made no answer, and left me.

Several friends were in, during the day. While talking to them, I would, without thinking, put my hand into my bosom, to show them my letter of authority. But I soon found, as my friends told me, it was in my heart, and was to be shown in my life, instead of in my hand. Among others, my minister, Jehial C. Beman, came to see me. He looked very coldly upon me and said: "I guess you will find out your mistake before you are many months older." He was a scholar, and a fine speaker; and the sneering, indifferent way in which he addressed me, said most plainly:

"You don't know anything." I replied: "My
gifts are very small, I know, but I can no
longer be shaken by what you or any one else
may think or say."

CHAPTER XIX.

Public Effort—Excommunication.

FROM this time the opposition to my life-
work commenced, instigated by the minister,
Mr. Beman. Many in the church were anxious to have me preach in the hall, where our
meetings were held at that time, and were not
a little astonished at the minister's cool treat-
ment of me. At length two of the trustees got
some of the elder sisters to call on the minister
and ask him to let me preach. His answer
was: "No; she can't preach her holiness stuff
here, and I am astonished that you should ask
it of me." The sisters said he seemed to be in
quite a rage, although he said he was not
angry.

There being no meeting of the society on
Monday evening, a brother in the church

opened his house to me, that I might preach,
which displeased Mr. Beman very much. He
appointed a committee to wait upon the
brother and sister who had opened their doors
to me, to tell them they must not allow any
more meetings of that kind, and that they
must abide by the rules of the church, making
them believe they would be excommunicated
if they disobeyed him. I happened to be
present at this interview, and the committee
remonstrated with me for the course I had
taken. I told them my business was with the
Lord, and wherever I found a door opened I
intended to go in and work for my Master.

There was another meeting appointed at the
same place, which I, of course, attended; after
which the meetings were stopped for that
time, though I held many more there after
these people had withdrawn from Mr. Beman's
church.

I then held meetings in my own house;
whereat the minister told the members that
if they attended them he would deal with
them, for they were breaking the rules of the
church. When he found that I continued the
meetings, and that the Lord was blessing my
feeble efforts, he sent a committee of two to ask
me if I considered myself a member of his
church. I told them I did, and should con-

tinue to do so until I had done something worthy of dismembership.

At this, Mr. Beman sent another committee with a note, asking me to meet him with the committee, which I did. He asked me a number of questions, nearly all of which I have forgotten. One, however, I do remember: he asked if I was willing to comply with the rules of the discipline. To this I answered: "Not if the discipline prohibits me from doing what God has bidden me to do; I fear God more than man." Similar questions were asked and answered in the same manner. The committee said what they wished to say, and then told me I could go home. When I reached the door, I turned and said: "I now shake off the dust of my feet as a witness against you. See to it that this meeting does not rise in judgment against you."

The next evening, one of the committee came to me and told me that I was no longer a member of the church, because I had violated the rules of the discipline by preaching.

When this action became known, the people wondered how any one could be excommunicated for trying to do good. I did not say much, and my friends simply said I had done nothing but hold meetings. Others, anxious to know the particulars, asked the minister what the trouble was. He told them he had given me the privilege of speaking or preaching as long as I chose, but that he could not give me the right to use the pulpit, and that I was not satisfied with any other place. Also, that I had appointed meeting on the evening of his meetings, which was a thing no member had a right to do. For these reasons he said he had turned me out of the church.

Now, if the people who repeated this to me told the truth—and I have no doubt but they did—Mr. Beman told an actual falsehood. I had never asked for his pulpit, but had told him and others, repeatedly, that I did not care where I stood—any corner of the hall would do. To which Mr. Beman had answered: "You cannot have any place in the hall." Then I said: "I'll preach in a private house." He answered me: "No, not in this place; I am stationed over all Boston." He was determined I should not preach in the city of Boston. To cover up his deceptive, unrighteous course toward me, he told the above falsehoods.

From his statements, many erroneous stories concerning me gained credence with a large number of people. At that time, I thought it my duty as well as privilege to address a letter to the Conference, which I took to them in person, stating all the facts. At the same time I told them it was not in the power of Mr. Beman, or any one else, to truthfully bring anything against my moral or religious character—that my only offence was in trying to preach the Gospel of Christ—and that I cherished no ill feelings toward Mr. Beman or any one else, but that I desired the Conference to give the case an impartial hearing, and then give me a written statement expressive of their opinion. I also said I considered myself a member of the Conference, and should do so until they said I was not, and gave me their reasons, that I might let the world know what my offence had been.

My letter was slightingly noticed, and then thrown under the table. Why should they notice it? It was only the grievance of a woman, and there was no justice meted out to women in those days. Even ministers of Christ did not feel that women had any rights which they were bound to respect.

CHAPTER XX.

Women in the Gospel.

THIRTY years ago there could scarcely a person be found, in the churches, to sympathize with any one who talked of Holiness. But, in my simplicity, I did think that a body of Christian ministers would understand my case and judge righteously. I was, however, disappointed.

It is no little thing to feel that every man's hand is against us, and ours against every man, as seemed to be the case with me at this time; yet how precious, if Jesus but be with us. In this severe trial I had constant access to God, and a clear consciousness that he heard me; yet I did not seem to have that plenitude of the Spirit that I had before. I realized most keenly that the closer the communion that may have existed, the keener the suffering of the slightest departure from God. Unbroken communion can only be retained by a constant application of the blood which cleanseth.

Though I did not wish to pain any one, neither could I please any one only as I was led by the Holy Spirit. I saw, as never before, that the best men were liable to err, and that the only safe way was to fall on Christ, even though censure and reproach fell upon me for obeying his voice. Man's opinion weighed nothing with me, for my commission was from heaven, and my reward was with the Most High.

I could not believe that it was a short-lived impulse or spasmodic influence that impelled me to preach. I read that on the day of Pentecost was the Scripture fulfilled as found in Joel ii. 28, 29; and it certainly will not be denied that women as well as men were at that time filled with the Holy Ghost, because it is expressly stated that women were among those who continued in prayer and supplication, waiting for the fulfillment of the promise. Women and men are classed together, and if the power to preach the Gospel is short-lived and spasmodic in the case of women, it must be equally so in that of men; and if women have lost the gift of prophecy, so have men.

We are sometimes told that if a woman pretends to a Divine call, and thereon grounds the right to plead the cause of a crucified Redeemer in public, she will be believed when she shows credentials from heaven; that is, when she works a miracle. If it be necessary to prove one's right to preach the Gospel, I ask of my brethren to show me their credentials, or I can not believe in the propriety of their ministry.

But the Bible puts an end to this strife when it says: "There is neither male nor female in Christ Jesus." Philip had four daughters that prophesied, or preached. Paul called Priscilla, as well as Aquila, his "helper," or, as in the Greek, his "fellow-laborer." Rom. xv. 3; 2 Cor. viii. 23; Phil. ii. 5; 1 Thess. iii. 2. The same word, which, in our common translation, is now rendered a "servant of the church," in speaking of Phebe (Rom. xix. 1.), is rendered "minister" when applied to Tychicus. Eph. vi. 21. When Paul said, "Help those women who labor with me in the Gospel," he certainly meant that they did more than to pour out tea. In the eleventh chapter of First Corinthians Paul gives directions, to men and women, how they should appear when they prophesy or pray in public assemblies; and he defines prophesying to be speaking to edification, exhortation and comfort.

I may further remark that the conduct of holy women is recorded in Scripture as an example to others of their sex. And in the early ages of Christianity many women were happy and glorious in martyrdom. How nobly, how heroically, too, in later ages, have women suffered persecution and death for the name of the Lord Jesus.

In looking over these facts, I could see no miracle wrought for those women more than in myself.

Though opposed, I went forth laboring for God, and he owned and blessed my labors, and has done so wherever I have been until this day. And while I walk obediently, I know he will, though hell may rage and vent its spite.

CHAPTER XXI.

The Lord Leadeth—Labor in Philadelphia.

As I left the Conference, God wonderfully filled my heart with his love, so that, as I passed from place to place, meeting one and another of the ministers, my heart went out in love to each of them as though he had been my father; and the language of 1 Pet. i. 7, came forcibly to my mind: "The trial of our faith is much more precious than of gold that perisheth, though it be tried by fire." Fiery trials are not strange things to the Lord's anointed. The rejoicing in them is born only of the Holy Spirit. Oh, praise his holy name for a circumcised heart, teaching us that each trial of our faith hath its commission from the Father of spirits. Each wave of trial bears the Galilean Pilot on its crest. Listen: his voice is in the storm, and winds and waves obey that voice: "It is I; be not afraid." He has promised us help and safety in the fires, and not escape from them.

(6)

"And hereby we know that he abideth in us, by the Spirit which he hath given us." 1 John iii. 24. Glory to the Lamb for the witness of the Holy Spirit! He knoweth that every step I have taken has been for the glory of God and the good of souls. However much I may have erred in judgment, it has been the fault of my head and not of my heart. I sleep, but my heart waketh; bless the Lord.

Had this opposition come from the world, it would have seemed as nothing. But coming, as it did, from those who had been much blessed—blessed with me—and who had once been friends of mine, it touched a tender spot; and had it not been for the precious blood of Jesus, I should have been lost.

While in Philadelphia, attending the Conference, I became acquainted with three sisters who believed they were called to public labors in their Master's vineyard. But they had been so opposed, they were very much distressed and shrank from their duty. One of them professed sanctification. They had met with more opposition from ministers than from any one else.

After the Conference had adjourned, I proposed to these sisters to procure a place and hold a series of meetings. They were pleased with the idea, and were willing to help if I

would take charge of the meetings. They
apprehended some difficulty, as there had
never been a meeting there under the sole
charge of women. The language of my heart
was:

"Only Thou my Leader be
And I still will follow Thee."

Trusting in my Leader, I went on with the
work. I hired a large place in Canal street,
and there we opened our meetings, which continued eleven nights, and over one Sabbath.
The room was crowded every night—some
coming to receive good, others to criticise,
sneer, and say hard things against us.

One of the sisters left us after a day or two,
fearing that the Church to which she belonged
would disown her if she continued to assist us.
We regretted this very much, but could only
say, "An enemy hath done this."

These meetings were a time of refreshing
from the presence of the Lord. Many were
converted, and a few stepped into the fountain
of cleansing.

Some of the ministers, who remained in the
city after the Conference, attended our meetings, and occasionally asked us if we were
organizing a new Conference, with a view of
drawing out from the churches. This was
simply to ridicule our meeting.

We closed with a love-feast, which caused such a stir among the ministers and many of the church-members, that we could not imagine what the end would be. They seemed to think we had well nigh committed the unpardonable sin.

CHAPTER XXII.

A Visit to my Parents—Further Labors.

SOME of the dear sisters accompanied me to Flatbush, where I assisted in a bush meeting. The Lord met the people in great power, and I doubt not there are many souls in glory to-day praising God for that meeting.

From that place I went home to my father's house in Binghamton, N. Y. They were filled with joy to have me with them once more, after an absence of six years. As my mother embraced me, she exclaimed: "So you are a preacher, are you?" I replied: "So they say." "Well, Julia," said she, "when I first heard that you were a preacher, I said that I would rather hear you were dead." These words, coming so unexpectedly from my mother, filled me with anguish. Was I to meet opposition here, too? But my mother, with streaming eyes, continued: "My dear daughter, it is all past now. I have heard from those who have attended your meetings what the Lord has done for you, and I am satisfied."

My stay in Binghamton was protracted several months. I held meetings in and around the town, to the acceptance of the people, and, I trust, to the glory of God. I felt perfectly satisfied, when the time came for me to leave, that my work was all for the Lord, and my soul was filled with joy and thankfulness for salvation. Before leaving, my parents decided to move to Boston, which they did soon after.

I left Binghamton the first of February, 1855, in company with the Rev. Henry Johnson and his wife, for Ithaca, N. Y., where I labored a short time. I met with some opposition from one of the A. M. E. Church trustees. He said a woman should not preach in the church. Beloved, the God we serve fights all our battles, and before I left the place that trustee was one of the most faithful at my meetings, and was very kind to assist me on my journey when I left Ithaca. I stopped one night at Owego, at Brother Loyd's, and I also stopped for a short time at Onondaga, returned to Ithaca on the 14th of February, and staid until the 7th of March, during which time the work of grace was greatly revived. Some believed and entered into the rest of full salvation, many were converted, and a number of backsliders were reclaimed. I held prayer-meetings from house to house. The sisters formed a woman's prayer-meeting, and the whole church seemed to be working in unison for Christ.

March 7th I took the stage for Geneva, and, arriving late at night, went to a hotel. In the morning Brother Rosel Jeffrey took me to his house and left me with his wife. He was a zealous Christian, but she scoffed at religion, and laughed and made sport during family worship. I do not know, but hope that long ere this she has ceased to ridicule the cause or the followers of Christ. In the latter part of the day Brother Condell came and invited me to his house. I found his wife a pleasant Christian woman. Sabbath afternoon I held a meeting in Brother Condell's house. The colored people had a church which the whites had given them. It was a union church, to be occupied on alternate Sundays by the Methodists and Baptists.

According to arrangement, this Sunday evening was the time for the Methodists to

occupy the church. The Rev. Dawsey, of Can-
andaigua, came to fill his appointment, but,
when we arrived at the church, the Baptist
minister, William Monroe, objected to our
holding a meeting in the house that evening,
and his members joined with him in his
unchristian course. Rather than have any
trouble, we returned to Brother Condell's
house. The minister preached and I followed
with a short exhortation. The Lord was present to bless. They made an appointment for
me to preach at the union meeting-house on
the following Tuesday evening.

Monday evening I went with some of the
sisters to the church, where there was a meeting for the purpose of forming a moral reform
society.

After the meeting, Brother Condell asked
the trustees if they had any objection to having me speak in the church the next evening.
To this, Minister Monroe and another man—I
had almost said a fiend in human shape—
answered that they did not believe in women's
preaching, and would not admit one in the
church, striving hard to justify themselves
from the Bible, which one of them held in his
unholy hands.

I arose to speak, when Mr. Monroe inter-
rupted me. After a few words I left the house.

The next afternoon, while taking tea at the house of one of the sisters, Minister Monroe came in to tell me he heard that our brethren had said they would have the church for me if they had to "shed blood." He asked me if I wanted to have anything to do with a fight of that kind. I replied: "The weapons with which I fight are not carnal, and, if I go to a place and am invited to use the weapons God has given me, I must use them to his glory."

"Well," said he, "I shall be in the pulpit at an early hour, and will not leave it though they break my head."

"Mr. Monroe," said I, "God can take you from the pulpit without breaking your head." At this he became very much excited, and raved as if he were a madman. For two hours he walked the floor, talking and reading all the time. I made him no reply and tried not to notice him, and finally he left me.

At the proper time we went to the church. It was full, but everything was in confusion. Mr. Monroe was in the pulpit. I saw at once that God could not be glorified in the midst of such a pandemonium; so I withdrew at once. I was told they kept up the contention until after ten o'clock. Mr. Monroe tried hard to get our trustees to say I should not preach in the place, but they would give him no such promise.

As I was obliged to leave in a few days, to meet other appointments, our men procured a large house, where I held a meeting the next evening. All that attended were quiet and orderly; one man arose for prayers.

Dear sisters, who are in the evangelistic work now, you may think you have hard times; but let me tell you, I feel that the lion and lamb are lying down together, as compared with the state of things twenty-five or thirty years ago. Yes, yes; our God is marching on. Glory to his name!

CHAPTER XXIII.

Indignities on Account of Color—General Conference.

I REACHED Rochester on the 16th of March, where I remained three weeks, laboring constantly for my Master, who rewarded me in the salvation of souls. Here God visited me after the same manner he did Elijah, when Elijah prayed to die. He strengthened me and bid me go forward with the promises recorded in the first chapter of Joshua.

April 21st I bade good-bye to Brother John H. Bishop's people, who had entertained me while in Rochester, and went to Binghamton to visit my parents again. I found them all well, and labored constantly for the Lord while I was there. I remained at home until the 8th of May, when I once more started out on my travels for the Lord. There was but one passenger in the stage besides myself. He gave his name as White, seemed very uneasy, and, at each stopping place, he would say: "I am afraid the public will take me for an aboli-

tionist to-day;" thus showing his dark, slave-
holding principles.

I staid one night in Oxford, at Mr. Jack-
son's. At six o'clock the next morning I took
passage on the canal packet "Governor Sew-
ard," with Captain George Keeler. That night,
at a late hour, I made my way into the ladies'
cabin, and, finding an empty berth, retired.
In a short time a man came into the cabin,
saying that the berths in the gentlemen's
cabin were all occupied, and he was going to
sleep in the ladies' cabin. Then he pointed
to me and said: "That nigger has no business
here. My family are coming on board the
boat at Utica, and they shall not come where a
nigger is." They called the captain, and he
ordered me to get up; but I did not stir, thinking it best not to leave the bed except by force.
Finally they left me, and the man found lodging among the seamen, swearing vengeance on
the "niggers."

The next night the boat stopped at a vil-
lage, and the captain procured lodging for me
at an inn. Thus I escaped further abuse from
that ungodly man.

The second night we reached Utica, where I
staid over Sunday. Then I went to Schenectady, where I remained a few days, working for
my Master. Then I went to Albany, my old

home. Sunday afternoon I preached in Troy, and that Sunday evening in Albany, to a crowded house. There were many of my old friends and acquaintances in the audience. This was the most solemn and interesting meeting I ever held. The entire audience seemed moved to prayer and tears by the power of the Holy Ghost.

On May 21st I went to New York. During the year that followed I visited too large a number of places to mention in this little work.

I went from Philadelphia in company with thirty ministers and Bishop Brown, to attend the General Conference, which was held in Pittsburgh, Pa. The ministers chartered the conveyance, and we had a very pleasant and interesting journey. The discussions during the day and meetings at night, on the canal boat, were instructive and entertaining. A very dear sister, Ann M. Johnson, accompanied me. The grand, romantic scenery, which I beheld while crossing the Alleghany mountains, filled me with adoration and praise to the great Creator of all things. We reached Pittsburgh on the 4th of June, and the General Conference of the A. M. E. Church convened on the 6th of June. The Conference lasted two weeks, and was held with open doors.

The business common to such meetings was transacted with spirit and harmony, with few exceptions. One was, a motion to prevent Free Masons from ministering in the churches. Another, to allow all the women preachers to become members of the conferences. This caused quite a sensation, bringing many members to their feet at once. They all talked and screamed to the bishop, who could scarcely keep order. The Conference was so incensed at the brother who offered the petition that they threatened to take action against him.

I remained several weeks, laboring among the people, much to the comfort of my own soul, and, I humbly trust, to the upbuilding of my dear Master's kingdom. I found the people very kind and benevolent.

CHAPTER XXIV.

Continued Labors—Death of my Husband and Father.

FROM Pittsburgh I went to Cincinnati, where I found a large number of colored people of different denominations. The Methodists had a very good meeting-house on Sixth street, below Broad street. The members appeared to enjoy religion, but were very much like the world in their external appearance and cold indifference toward each other.

The station and circuit joined in holding a camp-meeting. The minister urged me very strongly to attend, which I did. Several souls professed faith in Christ at this meeting, but only one was willing to receive him in all his fullness.

After this meeting I labored in quite a number of places in Ohio. At some places I was kindly received, at others I was not allowed to labor publicly.

While thus laboring far from home, the sad intelligence of my husband's death came to me

so suddenly as to almost cause me to sink
beneath the blow. But the arm of my dear,
loving, heavenly Father sustained me, and I
was enabled to say: "Though he slay me, yet
will I trust in him." I immediately hastened
home to Boston, where I learned the particulars of my husband's death, which occurred on
ship-board several months before. None but
the dear Lord knew what my feelings were. I
dared not complain, and thus cast contempt on
my blessed Saviour, for I knew he would not
lay more upon me than I could bear. He
knows how to deliver the godly out of temptation and affliction; all events belong to him.
All we have to be careful for is, to know of a
truth that Christ is formed in our hearts the
hope of glory, and hath set up his kingdom
there, to reign over every affection and desire.
Glory to the Lamb, who giveth me power thus
to live!

After arranging my affairs at home, I went
to Albany, where my sister lived, staid a short
time with her, and held some meetings there.
Then I went to Bethlehem, where I held several meetings, one in the M. E. Church, which
was arranged only after there had been con-
siderable controversy about letting a woman
preach in their house. From there I went to
Troy, where I also held meetings. In each of

these places this "brand plucked from the burning" was used of God to his glory in saving precious souls. To his name be all the glory!

I spent one Sunday in Poughkeepsie, working for Jesus. I then went to New York, where I took the boat for Boston. We were detained some hours by one of the shafts breaking. I took a very severe cold by being compelled to sit on deck all night, in the cold, damp air—prejudice not permitting one of my color to enter the cabin except in the capacity of a servant. O Prejudice! thou cruel monster! wilt thou ever cease to exist? Not until all shall know the Lord, and holiness shall be written upon the bells of the horses—upon all things in earth as well as in heaven. Glory to the Lamb, whose right it is to reign!

Upon my arrival home I found my father quite ill. He was sick for several months, and I remained at home until after his death, which event took place in May, 1849. He bore his long, painful illness with Christian patience and resignation. Just before leaving us for the better world, he called each of his children that were present to his bedside, exhorting them to live here in such a manner that they might meet him in heaven. To me he said: "My dear daughter, be faithful to your heavonly calling, and fear not to preach full salvation." After some precious words to his weeping wife, my dear father was taken to his eternal rest. Bless the Lord, O my soul, for an earnest, Christian father! Reader, I trust it is your lot to have faithful, believing parents.

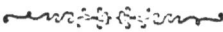

CHAPTER XXV.

Work in Various Places.

June 18th, 1849, I bade my mother and family farewell, and started out on my mission again. I stopped in New York, where I was joined by Sister Ann M. Johnson, who became my traveling companion. We went to Philadelphia, where we were entertained by Brother and Sister Lee. The dear, kind friends welcomed us warmly. Sister Johnson did not feel moved to labor in public, except to sing, pray, and recount her experience. I labored constantly while in this city, going from church to church.

On the 28th we went to Snow Hill, where we spent one Sunday. We visited Fethers-

ville, Bordentown, Westchester and Westtown,
all to the glory of God. I must say, the dear
Holy Spirit wonderfully visited the people in
all these places. Many were converted, and,
now and then, one would step into the fountain of cleansing.

July 20th we left for New York, stopping
at Burlington, Trenton, Princeton, Rahway,
Brunswick and Newark. In each of these
places we spent several days, much to our comfort and the apparent good of the churches.
We arrived in New York city August 3d, and
went to Bridgeport (Conn.) by boat. We
found the church there in a very unsettled
condition because of unbelief. We next went
to New Haven, where we had some precious
meetings. In Providence, R. I., we also received
God's blessing on our labors.

At this time I received a pressing invitation
from Rev. Daniel A. Paine, who is now bishop
of the A. M. E. Church, to visit Baltimore,
which I accepted. Upon our arrival there we
were closely questioned as to our freedom, and
carefully examined for marks on our persons
by which to identify us if we should prove to
be runaways. While there, a daughter of the
lady with whom we boarded ran away from
her self-styled master. He came, with others,
to her mother's house at midnight, burst in

the door without ceremony, and swore the girl
was hid in the house, and that he would have
her, dead or alive. They repeated this for
several nights. They often came to our bed
and held their light in our faces, to see if the
one for whom they were looking was not with
us. The mother was, of course, in great distress. I believe they never recovered the girl.
Thank the dear Lord we do not have to suffer
such indignities now, though the monster,
Slavery, is not yet dead in all its forms.

We remained some time in Baltimore, laboring mostly in Brother Paine's charge. We
then went to Washington, D. C., where our
Conference was in session. The meetings were
excellent, and great good was being done,
when an incident occurred which cast a gloom
over the whole Conference. One day, when a
number of the ministers, Sister Johnson and
myself, were dining at the house of one of the
brethren, a slaveholder came and searched the
house for a runaway. We realized more and
more what a terrible thing it was for one
human being to have absolute control over
another.

We remained in Washington a few weeks,
laboring for Christ. Although, at the time, it
seemed as though Satan ruled there supreme,
God gave us to know that his righteousness

was being set up in many hearts. Glory to his excellent name.

The larger portion of the past year had been a time of close trial, yet I do not recollect ever closing a year more fully in Christ than I did that one. On taking a retrospective view of it, I found great cause for humiliation as well as thankfulness. I was satisfied with the Lord's dealings with me; my mind was kept in peace, while many had declined on the right hand and on the left; I was thankful that any were spared to bear the standard of the Redeemer.

Since I first entered the vineyard of my divine Master, I have seen many a star fall, and many a shining light go out and sink into darkness. Many, who have been singularly owned and blessed of God, have deserted his standard in the day of trial ; yet, through his abounding grace, have I been kept. Glory be to the keeping power of the blood that cleanseth me, even me, from all sin!

CHAPTER XXVI.

Further Labors—A "Threshing" Sermon.

In June, 1850, I crossed the Alleghany mountains the second time. I was very sick on the journey, and on arriving in Pittsburgh, was not able to sit up. Finding me in a raging fever, my friends called in a physician, and, as I continued to grow worse, another one. For three weeks my life was despaired of; and finally, on beginning to recover, it was many months before I felt quite well. In this severe affliction grace wonderfully sustained me. Bless the Lord!

I was advised to go down the Ohio river for the benefit of my health. Therefore, as soon as I was able to do so, I started for Cincinnati. I staid there several weeks with some friends by the name of Jones. The Lord so strengthened me, that, in a few months, I was able to resume my labors.

In October we went to Columbus. We labored there and in that vicinity for some time, content that in our protracted effort quite a number were converted. There were three persons there who said they had once enjoyed the blessing of sanctification, but were not then clear in the experience. Oh, how few are advocates for full salvation! Some will hold the whole truth in profession when and where it is not opposed, but, if they must become fools for the truth's sake, they compromise with error. Such have not and will not come to the perfect rest and inheritance of the saints on earth.

In April, 1851, we visited Chillicothe, and had some glorious meetings there. Great crowds attended every night, and the altar was crowded with anxious inquirers. Some of the deacons of the white people's Baptist church invited me to preach in their church, but I declined to do so, on account of the opposition of the pastor, who was very much set against women's preaching. He said so much against it, and against the members who wished me to preach, that they called a church meeting, and I heard that they finally dismissed him.

The white Methodists invited me to speak for them, but did not want the colored people to attend the meeting. I would not agree to any such arrangement, and, therefore, I did

not speak for them. Prejudice had closed the
door of their sanctuary against the colored
people of the place, virtually saying: "The
Gospel shall not be free to all." Our benign
Master and Saviour said: "Go, preach my Gospel to all."

We visited Zanesville, Ohio, laboring for
white and colored people. The white Methodists opened their house for the admission of
colored people for the first time. Hundreds
were turned away at each meeting, unable to
get in; and, although the house was so crowded,
perfect order prevailed. We also held meetings on the other side of the river. God the
Holy Ghost was powerfully manifest in all
these meetings. I was the recipient of many
mercies, and passed through various exercises.
In all of them I could trace the hand of God
and claim divine assistance whenever I most
needed it. Whatever I needed, by faith I had.
Glory! glory!! While God lives, and Jesus
sits on his right hand, nothing shall be impossible unto me, if I hold fast faith with a pure
conscience.

On the 27th we went to Detroit, Mich. On
the way, Sister Johnson had a very severe
attack of ague, which lasted for several weeks.
My soul had great liberty for God while laboring in this place.

One day, quite an influential man in the community, though a sinner, called on me and appeared deeply concerned about his soul's welfare. He urged me to speak from Micah iv. 13: "Arise and thresh, O daughter of Zion," etc. I took his desire to the Lord, and was permitted to speak from that passage after this manner: 710 B. C. corn was threshed among the Orientals by means of oxen or horses, which were driven round an area filled with loose sheaves. By their continued tramping the corn was separated from the straw. That this might be done the more effectually, the text promised an addition to the natural horny substance on the feet of these animals, by making the horn iron and the hoof brass.

Corn is not threshed in this manner by us, but by means of flails, so that I feel I am doing no injury to the sentiment of the text by changing a few of the terms into those which are the most familiar to us now. The passage portrays the Gospel times, though in a more restricted sense it applies to the preachers of the word. Yet it has a direct reference to all God's people, who were and are commanded to arise and thresh. Glory to Jesus! now is this prophecy fulfilled—Joel ii. 28 and 29. They are also commanded to go to God, who alone is able to qualify them for their labors by making their horns iron and their hoofs brass. The Lord was desirous of imparting stability and perpetuity to his own divine work, by granting supernatural aid to the faithful that they might perform for him those services for which their own feeble and unassisted powers were totally inadequate. More than this, it is encouraging to the saints to know that they are provided with weapons both offensive and defensive.

The threshing instrument is of the former description. It is of the same quality as that which is quick and powerful and sharper than any two-edged sword. "For this purpose the Son of God was manifested, that he might destroy the works of the devil," and this is one of the weapons which he employs in the hands of his people to carry his gracious designs into execution, together with the promise that they shall beat in pieces many people. Isa. xxiii. 18; lx. 6–9.

There are many instances of the successful application of the Gospel flail, by which means the devil is threshed out of sinners. With the help of God, I am resolved, O sinner, to try what effect the smart strokes of this threshing instrument will produce on thy unhumbled soul. This is called the sword of the Spirit, and is in reality the word of God.

Such a weapon may seem contemptible in the eyes of the natural man; yet, when it is powerfully wielded, the consequences are invariably potent and salutary. Bless God! the Revelator says: "They overcame by the blood of the Lamb and by the word of their testimony; and they loved not their lives unto the death." The atonement is the greatest weapon. In making trial of its efficacy, little children have caused the parent to cry aloud for mercy; but, in every case, much of its heavenly charm and virtue depends upon the mode in which it is applied.

This Gospel flail should be lifted up in a kind and loving spirit. Many shrink at sight of the flail, and some of us know, by blessed experience, that when its smart strokes are applied in the power and demonstration of the Holy Spirit, it causes the very heart to feel sore and painful. Penitent soul, receive the castigation, and you will feel, after it, like saying: "Now let me be crucified, and this work of the devil, inbred sin, put to death, that Christ may live and reign in me without a rival."

To the glory of God I wish to say, that the unconverted man, who gave me the text for the above discourse, gave his heart to God, together with many others, before we left

Detroit. In after years I was informed of his happy death. Praise the Lord for full and free salvation! Reader, have you this salvation—an ever-flowing fountain—in your soul? God grant it. Amen!

CHAPTER XXVII.

My Cleveland Home—Later Labors.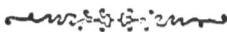

In June, 1851, we went to Canada, where we were kindly received. We labored in different churches with great success. We found many living Christians there—some holding high the light of full salvation, and others willing to be cleansed. After spending a few weeks there, we crossed to Buffalo, but did not make any stay there at that time.

The places visited during that year are too numerous to mention here. Suffice it to say, the great Head of the Church went before us, clearing the way and giving us unmistakable evidence of his presence in every battle. Hallelujah!

We returned to Columbus to fill an appointment which was awaiting us. After this, we made arrangements to go to Cleveland. One of the brethren engaged our passage and paid the fare, but we were not permitted to leave until four days afterward. At that time a colored person was not allowed to ride in the stage if any white passenger objected to it. There were objections made for three mornings, but, on the fourth, the stage called for us, and we had a safe journey to Cleveland. We expected to make a visit only, as in other cities; but the All-Father intended otherwise, and, more than twenty years ago, Cleveland became my home. After settling down, we still continued to visit neighboring cities and labor for Christ.

It was about this time that I became afflicted with the throat difficulty, of which I shall speak later. Beloved, the dear Lord only knows how sorely I was tried and tempted over this affliction.

St. James speaks of temptations as being common to the most holy of men, and also as a matter of joy and rejoicing to such as are exercised thereby, if so be they are not overcome by them. I think all temptation has a tendency to sin, but all temptation is not sin. There is a diversity of temptations, and a diversity of causes from which temptations proceed. Some come immediately from our corrupt nature, and are in themselves sinful. Others arise from the infirmity of our nature, and these every Christian has to contend with so long as he sojourns in a tabernacle of clay. There are also temptations which come directly from the enemy of souls. These our blessed Lord severely labored under, and so do the majority of his children. " Blessed is the man that endureth temptation"!

During the years that I rested from my labors and tried to recover my health, God permitted me to pass through the furnace of trial, heated seven times hotter than usual. Had not the three-one God been with me, I surely must have gone beneath the waves. God permits afflictions and persecutions to come upon his chosen people to answer various ends. Sometimes for the trial of their faith, and the exercise of their patience and resignation to his will, and sometimes to draw them off from all human dependence, and to teach them to trust in Him alone. Sometimes he suffers the wicked to go a great way, and the ungodly to triumph over us, that he may prove our steadfastness and make manifest his power in upholding us. Thus it was with me. I had trusted too much in human wisdom, and

God suffered all these things to come upon me. He upheld me by his grace, freeing me from all care or concern about my health or what man could do. He taught me to sit patiently, and wait to hear my Shepherd's voice; for I was resolved to follow no stranger, however plausibly he might plead.

I shall praise God through all eternity for sending me to Cleveland, even though I have been called to suffer.

In 1856, Sister Johnson, who had been my companion during all these years of travel, left me for her heavenly home. She bore her short illness without a murmur, resting on Jesus. As she had lived, so she died, in the full assurance of faith, happy and collected to the last, maintaining her standing in the way of holiness without swerving either to the right or to the left. Glory to the blood that keeps us!

My now sainted mother, who was then in feeble health, lived with me in Cleveland for a few years. As the time for her departure drew near, she very much desired to visit her two daughters—one in Albany, the other in Boston. I feared she was not able to endure the journey, but her desire was so strong, and her confidence in God so great that he would spare her to see her girls again, that I finally con-

sented that she should undertake the journey.
I put her in charge of friends who were going
east, and she reached my sister's house in
safety. She had been with them but a few
weeks, when she bade them a long farewell
and passed peacefully to heaven. I shall see
her again where parting is unknown.

The glorious wave of holiness, which has
been rolling through Ohio during the past few
years, has swept every hindrance out of my
way, and sent me to sea once more with chart
and compass.

"The Bible is my chart; it is a chart and compass too,
Whose needle points forever true."

When I drop anchor again, it will be in
heaven's broad bay.

Glory to Jesus for putting into my hand
that precious, living light, *"The Christian Harvester."* May it and its self-sacrificing editor
live many years, reflecting holy light as they
go.

If any one arise from the perusal of this
book, scoffing at the word of truth which he
has read, I charge him to prepare to answer
for the profanation at the peril of his soul.

CHAPTER XXVIII.

A Word to my Christian Sisters.

DEAR SISTERS: I would that I could tell you a hundredth part of what God has revealed to me of his glory, especially on that never-to-be-forgotten night when I received my high and holy calling. The songs I heard I think were those which Job, David and Isaiah speak of hearing at night upon their beds, or the one of which the Revelator says "no man could learn." Certain it is, I have not been able to sing it since, though at times I have seemed to hear the distant echo of the music. When I tried to repeat it, it vanished in the dim distance. Glory! glory! glory to the Most High!

Sisters, shall not you and I unite with the heavenly host in the grand chorus? If so, you will not let what man may say or do, keep you from doing the will of the Lord or using the gifts you have for the good of others. How much easier to bear the reproach of men

than to live at a distance from God. Be not
kept in bondage by those who say, "We suffer
not a woman to teach," thus quoting Paul's
words, but not rightly applying them. What
though we are called to pass through deep
waters, so our anchor is cast within the veil,
both sure and steadfast? Blessed experience!
I have had to weep because this was not my
constant experience. At times, a cloud of
heaviness has covered my mind, and disobedi-
ence has caused me to lose the clear witness of
perfect love.

One time I allowed my mind to dwell too
much on my physical condition. I was suffering severely from throat difficulty, and took
the advice of friends, and sought a cure from
earthly physicians, instead of applying to the
Great Physician. For this reason my joy was
checked, and I was obliged to cease my public
labors for several years. During all this time
I was less spiritual, less zealous, yet I was not
willing to accept the suggestion of Satan, that
I had forfeited the blessing of holiness. But
alas! the witness was not clear, and God suffered me to pass through close trials, tossed by
the billows of temptation.

Losing my loving husband just at this time,
I had much of the world to struggle with and
against.

(8)

Those who are wholly sanctified need not fear that God will hide his face, if they continue to walk in the light even as Christ is in the light. Then they have fellowship with the Father and the Son, and become of one spirit with the Lord. I do not believe God ever withdraws himself from a soul which does not first withdraw itself from him, though such may abide under a cloud for a season, and have to cry: "My God! my God! why hast thou forsaken me?"

Glory to God, who giveth us the victory through our Lord Jesus Christ! His blood meets all the demands of the law against us. It is the blood of Christ that sues for the fulfillment of his last will and testament, and brings down every blessing into the soul.

When I had well nigh despaired of a cure from my bodily infirmities, I cried from the depths of my soul for the blood of Jesus to be applied to my throat. My faith laid hold of the precious promises—John xiv. 14; Mark ii. 23; xi. 24. At once I ceased trying to join the iron and the clay—the truth of God with the sayings and advice of men. I looked to my God for a fresh act of his sanctifying power. Bless his name! deliverance did come, with the balm, and my throat has troubled me but little since. This was ten years ago. Praise

the Lord for that holy fire which many waters
of trial and temptation cannot quench.

Dear sisters in Christ, are any of you also
without understanding and slow of heart to
believe, as were the disciples? Although they
had seen their Master do many mighty works,
yet, with change of place or circumstances,
they would go back upon the old ground of
carnal reasoning and unbelieving fears. The
darkness and ignorance of our natures are
such, that, even after we have embraced the
Saviour and received his teaching, we are
ready to stumble at the plainest truths!
Blind unbelief is always sure to err; it can
neither trace God nor trust him. Unbelief is
ever alive to distrust and fear. So long as
this evil root has a place in us, our fears can
not be removed nor our hopes confirmed.

Not till the day of Pentecost did Christ's
chosen ones see clearly, or have their under-
standings opened; and nothing short of a full
baptism of the Spirit will dispel our unbelief.
Without this, we are but babes—all our lives
are often carried away by our carnal natures
and kept in bondage; whereas, if we are
wholly saved and live under the full sanctifying influence of the Holy Ghost, we cannot be
tossed about with every wind, but, like an iron
pillar or a house built upon a rock, prove

immovable. Our minds will then be fully illuminated, our hearts purified, and our souls filled with the pure love of God, bringing forth fruit to his glory.

CHAPTER XXIX.

Love not the World.

"IF any man love the world, the love of the Father is not in him." 1 John ii. 15. The spirit which is in the world is widely different from the Spirit which is of God; yet many vainly imagine they can unite the two. But as we read in Luke x. 26, so it is between the spirit of the world and the Spirit which is of God. There is a great gulf fixed between them—a gulf which cuts off all union and intercourse; and this gulf will eternally prevent the least degree of fellowship in spirit.

If we be of God and have the love of the Father in our hearts, we are not of the world, because whatsoever is of the world is not of God. We must be one or the other. We can not unite heaven and hell—light and dark-

ness. Worldly honor, worldly pleasure, worldly
grandeur, worldly designs and worldly pur-
suits are all incompatible with the love of the
Father and with that kingdom of righteousness, peace and joy in the Holy Ghost, which
is not of the world, but of God. Therefore,
God says: "Be not conformed to the world, but
be ye transformed by the renewing of your
mind, that ye may prove what is that good,
and acceptable. and perfect will of God."
Rom. xii. 2.

As we look at the professing Christians of
to-day, the question arises, Are they not all
conformed to the maxims and fashions of this
world, even many of those who profess to have
been sanctified? But they say the transform-
ing and renewing here spoken of means, as it
says, the mind, not the clothing. But, if the
mind be renewed, it must affect the clothing.
It is by the Word of God we are to be judged,
not by our opinion of the Word; hence, to the
law and the testimony. In a like manner the
Word also says: "That women adorn themselves in modest apparel, with shamefacedness
and sobriety, not with broidered hair, or gold,
or pearls, or costly array, but which becometh
a woman professing godliness, with good
works." 1 Tim. ii. 9, 10; 1 Pet. iii. 3–5. I
might quote many passages to the same effect,

if I had time or room. Will you not hunt them up, and read carefully and prayerfully for yourselves?

Dear Christians, is not the low state of pure religion among all the churches the result of this worldly-mindedness? There is much outward show; and doth not this outward show portend the sore judgments of God to be executed upon the ministers and members? Malachi ii. 7, says: "The priest's lips should keep knowledge," etc. But it is a lamentable fact that too many priests' lips speak vanity. Many profess to teach, but few are able to feed the lambs, while the sheep are dying for lack of nourishment and the true knowledge of salvation.

The priests' office being to stand between God and the people, they ought to know the mind of God toward his people — what the acceptable and perfect will of God is. Under the law, it was required that the priests should be without blemish—having the whole of the inward and outward man as complete, uniform and consistent as it was possible to be under that dispensation; thereby showing the great purity that is required by God in all those who approach near unto him. "Speak unto Aaron and his sons that they separate themselves," etc. The Lord here gives a charge to

the priests, under a severe penalty, that in all
their approaches they shall sanctify themselves. Thus God would teach his ministers
and people that he is a holy God, and will be
worshiped in the beauty of holiness by all
those who come into his presence.

Man may fill his office in the church out-
wardly, and God may in much mercy draw
nigh to the people when devoutly assembled
to worship him; but, if the minister has not
had previous recourse to the fountain which is
opened for sin and uncleanness, and felt the
sanctifying and renewing influences of the
Holy Ghost, he will feel himself shut out from
these divine communications. Oh, that God
may baptize the ministry and church with the
Holy Ghost and with fire.

By the baptism of fire the church must be
purged from its dead forms and notions respecting the inbeing of sin in all believers till
death. The Master said: "Now ye are clean
through the word which I have spoken unto
you; abide in me," etc. Oh! blessed union.
Christian, God wants to establish your heart
unblamable in holiness. 1 Thess. i. 13; iv. 7;
Heb. xii. 14; Rom. vi. 19. Will you let him
do it, by putting away all filthiness of the flesh
as well as of the spirit? "Know ye not that
ye are the temple of God?" etc. 1 Cor. iii. 16,

17; 2 Cor. vi. 16, 17. Thus we will continue to
search and find what the will of God is concerning his children. 1 Thess. iv. 3, 4. Bless
God! we may all have that inward, instanta-
neous sanctification, whereby the root, the
inbeing of sin, is destroyed.

Do not misunderstand me. I am not teaching absolute perfection, for that belongs to God
alone. Nor do I mean a state of angelic or
Adamic perfection, but Christian perfection—
an extinction of every temper contrary to
love.

"Now, the God of peace sanctify you wholly—
your whole spirit, soul and body. 2 Thess. v.
23. Glory to the blood!" "Faithful is he that
calleth you, who also will do it." Paul says:
He is able to do exceeding abundantly, above
all that we ask or think. Eph. iii. 20.

Beloved reader, remember that you cannot
commit sin and be a Christian, for "He that
committeth sin is of the devil." If you are
regenerated, sin does not reign in your mortal
body; but if you are sanctified, sin does not
exist in you. The sole ground of our perfect
peace from all the carnal mind is by the blood
of Jesus, for he is our peace, whom God hath
set forth to be a propiation, through faith in
his blood. "By whom also we have access by
faith into this grace wherein we stand"—hav-

ing entered into the holiest by the blood of
Jesus.

Let the blood be the sentinel, keeping the
tempter without, that you may have constant
peace within; for Satan cannot swim
waters. Isa. xxx. 7.

CHAPTER XXX.

How to Obtain Sanctification.

"MIXTURE of joy and sorrow
  I daily do pass through;
Sometimes I'm in the valley,
  Then sinking down with woe.

Chorus—Holy, holy, holy is the Lamb,
    Holy is the Lamb of God,
    Whose blood doth make me clean.

"Sometimes I am exalted,
  On eagle's wings I fly;
Rising above Mount Pisgah,
  I almost reach the sky.—*Chorus.*

"Sometimes I am in doubting,
  And think I have no grace;
Sometimes I am a-shouting,
  And camp-meeting is the place.—*Chorus.*

"Sometimes, when I am praying,
  It almost seems a task;
Sometimes I get a blessing,
  The greatest I can ask.—*Chorus.*

"Sometimes I read my Bible,
   It seems a sealed book;
Sometimes I find a blessing
   Wherever I do look.—*Chorus*

"Oh, why am I thus tossed—
   Thus tossed to and fro?
Because the blood of Jesus
   Hasn't washed me white as snow.—*Chorus*.

"Oh, come to Jesus now, and drink
   Of that holy, living stream;
Your thirst he'll quench, your soul revive,
   And cleanse you from all sin."—*Chorus*.

How is sanctification to be obtained? An important question. I answer, by faith. Faith is the only condition of sanctification. By this I mean a faith that dies out to the world and every form of sin; that gives up the sin of the heart; and that believes, according to God's promise, he is able to perform, and will do it now—doeth it now.

Why not yield, believe, and be sanctified now—now, while reading? "Now is the day of salvation." Say: "Here, Lord, I will, I do believe; thou hast said now—now let it be— now apply the blood of Jesus to my waiting, longing soul."

"Hallelujah! 'tis done!
  I believe on the Son;
  I am saved by the blood
  Of the crucified One."

Now, dear reader, I conclude by praying that this little work may be blessed of God to your spiritual and everlasting good. I trust also that it will promote the cause of holiness in the Church.

Now, unto Him who is able to do exceeding abundantly, above all that we ask or think, according to the power that worketh in us; unto Him be glory in the church by Christ Jesus throughout all ages, world without end. Amen.